This book belongs to:

_____

This paperback edition first published in 2020 by Andersen Press Ltd.
First published in Great Britain in 1987 by Andersen Press Ltd.,
20 Vauxhall Bridge Road, London SW1V 2SA.
Copyright © David McKee, 1987.
The right of David McKee to be identified as the author and illustrator of this work has been
asserted by him in accordance with the Copyright, Designs and Patents Act, 1988.
All rights reserved. Printed in China.

1   3   5   7   9   10   8   6   4   2

British Library Cataloguing in Publication Data available.

ISBN 978 1 78344 981 1

SNOW WOMAN

David McKee

ANDERSEN PRESS

"We're going to build a snowman," said Rupert.

"You mean a snowperson," said his father.

"We're going to build a snowman," said Rupert.

"You mean a snowperson," said his mother.

"I'm going to build a snow woman," said Kate.

"That's a good girl," said her mother.

"Snow woman? Nobody builds a snow woman,"
said Rupert. "We'll build a snowman."

"You can build a snowman, I'm going to build
a snow woman," said Kate.

Side by side they built their snowpeople.

Later they ran indoors again.

"I need a hat and scarf for the snowman," said Rupert.

"You mean snowperson," said his father.

"Can I have some clothes for the snow woman?" asked Kate.

"Certainly, dear," said Kate's mother, smiling.

They put the clothes on the snowpeople.

Then their mother took their photograph.

At bedtime, Rupert said, "Will the snowman be there in the morning?"

"You mean snowperson," said his father. "Yes, if it doesn't melt."

"Will the snow woman be there tomorrow?" asked Kate.

"I expect so, dear," said her mother.

"They've gone," gasped Rupert next morning.
"So have the clothes, so they didn't melt," said Kate.

"I've never heard of a snowman walking away before,"
said Rupert.

"Probably because he never had a snow woman before," said Kate. "Now what shall we do?"

"Let's build a snow bear," said Rupert.
"Man bear or lady bear?" asked Kate.

"Just a bear," said Rupert.

Read more David McKee classics:

Elmer

Not Now, Bernard

The Conquerors

Two Monsters

Tusk Tusk